Book One of

THE KLONDIKE KID

Trilogy

Sailing for Gold

By Deborah Hopkinson

Illustrated by Bill Farnsworth

ALADDIN
NEW YORK   LONDON   TORONTO   SYDNEY

For Donna, Kalā, and Shaun

First Aladdin Paperbacks edition March 2004

Text copyright © 2004 by Deborah Hopkinson
Illustrations copyright © 2004 by Bill Farnsworth

ALADDIN PAPERBACKS
An imprint of Simon & Schuster
Children's Publishing Division
1230 Avenue of the Americas
New York, NY 10020

Also available in an Aladdin library edition.
Designed by Sammy Yuen Jr.
The text of this book was set in Palatino.

Printed in the United States of America
2 4 6 8 10 9 7 5 3 1

Cataloging-in-Publication Data available from the Library of Congress

ISBN 0-689-86032-3 (library ed.)

8749

TABLE OF CONTENTS

Ho, for the Klondike,
Ho, for the Klondike,
Ho, for the Klondike, ho!

Put on your pack
And don't come back
Till you fill your sack
On the Northwest track.
Ho, ho, for the Klondike, ho!

∿ I Have a Secret Plan ∿

As soon as my chores were done, I rushed up the narrow stairs to my attic room and ran to the window.

It was only a tiny window. But from it, over the jumble of Seattle rooftops, I could see the waters of Puget Sound.

I spent hours alone here. Sometimes I sat with my pencil and paper, sketching the busy harbor or the snow-tipped mountains in the distance. Mostly, like now, I watched for boats.

Was that a steamship coming in? If only I had a pair of binoculars. I squinted to be sure.

Yes, a large steamship was headed for the docks.

I'd have to run down the hill to get there in time.

There was only one problem: Mrs. Tinker.

I tiptoed back down the stairs and into the hall, silent as a cat.

I was glad my shoes were old and worn. There wasn't a chance they'd squeak. The parlor door was closed. Maybe Mrs. Tinker was snoring away in her favorite chair.

At the door I grabbed the handle and turned it. *Slowly, slowly,* I told myself. My heart pounded like waves on a rock at high tide.

I pulled the door open, letting bright summer sun stream in. I picked up one foot and got ready to run. Almost free!

All at once I heard the click of sharp footsteps. The parlor door flew open.

Caught!

"Where do you think you're going, kid?"

growled Mrs. Tinker, grabbing my shirt with her fingernails.

Mrs. Tinker was tall and skinny. Whenever I looked at her I thought of a pencil—a sharp one.

My landlady leaned forward, her eyes glittering like tiny beads. "David Hill, why is it lately that every time I turn around, you're gone? Don't you have chores to do?"

I gulped. "I finished already, Mrs. Tinker. I helped Cook clean up after lunch, and I filled the wood bin."

I raised my voice, hoping Cook would hear. "Cook said I should go down to Pioneer Square to look for someone to rent Room Three, now that Mr. Jones is gone."

Mrs. Tinker let go of my shirt. "Humph. Don't you forget, I didn't have to let you stay on here after your mother died. Without me you'd be sleeping on the streets. And the streets of Seattle are rough for a ten-year-old boy."

"I'm eleven now, ma'am," I said in a low voice. "My birthday was last month, June fifteenth."

My birthday. At least Cook had remembered. She'd baked me a special cake with raisins. She'd even bought me a gift: a new pencil and some drawing paper. But it hadn't been the same without Momma.

Poor Momma. She'd been so sure we'd be happy in Seattle. "We'll start a new life here," she'd promised. "Everything is so green and fresh, not like New York."

Papa's death had left us poor, with not much more than our train fare. So Momma was happy to work as a maid for Mrs. Tinker. She cleaned the rooms, helped Cook, and served meals to the boarders. I liked listening to the men's stories of riding the rails across America, or sailing to faraway ports.

Mrs. Tinker had given Momma and me our own room in the attic. It wasn't much, but we were cozy together. Then the winter rains came. Momma caught a cold that wouldn't go away. By the time the doctor came, it was too late.

Just when I thought Mrs. Tinker wouldn't let me go, Cook stuck her head out of the kitchen. If Mrs. Tinker was hard and straight like a pencil, Cook was just the opposite. She reminded me of a soft, puffy biscuit, and she was always covered with flour.

"Oh, begging your pardon, ma'am," she said, wiping her large hands on her apron. "But I asked Davey to run downtown to find a nice gentleman who needs a place to stay. I'd go myself, but my knee pains me awful on the hills."

Cook winked, and I ducked my head to hide my grin.

Mrs. Tinker cuffed my ear. "All right, go on. But I don't want to hear you've gotten into any trouble. This town is full of ruffians, and I won't have one in my rooming house."

"Yes, ma'am," I said.

"And remember, I need this rooming house full to feed an extra mouth like you," she went on, leaning in so close I could smell the onions on her breath. "Don't expect supper if you don't bring back someone to rent Room Three."

I kept my head down. Truth was, I was a little afraid to look into those sharp eyes. I couldn't let Mrs. Tinker guess the real reason I headed downtown every chance I got.

I couldn't let her discover my secret plan.

CHAPTER TWO

∽ Waiting for Uncle Walt ∽

I scrambled out the back door and ran past the shed. No one except me ever went in it. That suited me just fine.

I sped through the backyard and around the house to the front. That's when I almost tripped over Joe. He raised his shiny black head and wagged his tail in a tired way.

Joe wasn't excited to see me. He was waiting for Mr. Tinker to come back. Ever since Mr. Tinker had left, Joe had kept watch for him. No one knew exactly where Mrs. Tinker's husband had gone. Some said he'd hopped a freight train to Chicago. Others said he'd sailed north to pan for gold.

Once, just before he disappeared, I'd heard Mr. Tinker talking softly to his dog. "My wife is as skinny as a carrot, and hard as one too," he told Joe. "I know she don't treat you well, but I thank you for being a good watchdog just the same."

Poor Joe. I could understand how he felt. The person I cared about most was gone too. I knew Momma could never come back.

But maybe my uncle Walt would.

One evening soon after Momma died, Cook had puffed her way up the attic stairs, bad knee and all.

"Davey, I'm awful sorry about your dear momma," she said, sinking down on my cot. She wiped her pink cheeks with her apron and panted a little. "But don't you have *any* other family? Seems to me your momma mentioned a brother."

"My uncle Walt," I told her. "But he's

always off on some adventure or another. He's gone to seek his fortune, like Mr. Tinker."

Cook closed her blue eyes. She always said she could think better with her eyes closed. "Hmm. But didn't he send you a letter once?"

"That's right. I almost forgot," I cried. "We got a letter around Christmas, right when Momma took sick. I . . . I was so scared then I don't think I paid much attention. I can't even remember where it was from."

"Let's look in that little wooden box your mother had," Cook suggested. "Maybe she kept it."

I opened the little box. The letter was there, right on top. "It's from a town in Alaska."

"Davey, I think you should write to your uncle Walt," Cook advised. "Ask him to come to Seattle to fetch you. After all, he's family. And family is what counts."

"What if he's left this town in Alaska already?" I asked Cook.

"Chances are, if he mailed letters from there once, sooner or later he'll pass back through the same town to check his mail," Cook assured me. "Just write your letter and wait."

I had. And ever since then I'd been waiting—and waiting. But there was no letter, and no sign of Uncle Walt.

Still, every time I saw a boat coming into the harbor, or every time the mail came, my heart beat faster. I couldn't help hoping Uncle Walt would write back—or even come straight to Seattle to get me. That's why I tried to be at the dock whenever a new boat arrived. And if the boat was from the frozen North, I made sure I talked to every man on board.

"Did you happen to meet my uncle up north, sir?" I'd say. "His name is Walt Thomas. He's a young fellow with dark hair."

But the men just shrugged or shook their heads.

As the months passed, and Uncle Walt didn't come, I began to give up hope. Maybe he'd never gotten my letter. Maybe he didn't know his only nephew was here, waiting.

That's when I came up with my secret plan.

Every chance I could, I went to Pioneer Square to earn a few pennies, a nickel, a dime, or even a quarter. I saved every cent I got.

When I had enough, I knew just what I would do: buy a boat ticket to Alaska.

If Uncle Walt wasn't coming to get me, well then, I'd just have to go find him.

I would have to run away.

CHAPTER THREE

∽ **Brownie's Secret** ∽

Mrs. Tinker's rooming house was perched on a Seattle hilltop. Running straight down the hill, I could be in Pioneer Square in ten minutes. If I didn't stop to pet Dandy.

Dandy belonged to our neighbor. Everyone called her Mrs. Mac.

"That horse is nothing but trouble," Mrs. Mac was always complaining. "Why, he's like a big dog. He gets into my flower beds and opens the gate. He even gets into the kitchen and devours my fresh apple pies!"

Today I called out as I ran by, "Hullo, Dandy. I'll bring you an apple soon. But you'd better be good for Mrs. Mac."

Dandy raised his head and chewed slowly on a bunch of daisies. I hoped daisies weren't Mrs. Mac's favorite flowers.

I didn't stop running until I got to Pioneer Square. It was a bustling, rowdy place. Even in tough times, like now, with men out of work, Pioneer Square always seemed full of possibility—and money to be made.

I hurried down Yesler Way to the docks. The steamer I'd spied from my window was already here. The first men were straggling down the gangplank, their legs shaky from long days at sea.

"Is this boat from Alaska?" I asked one man.

"Nope, kid. We came from the south, around Cape Horn," he replied.

My heart sank. No Uncle Walt today. Even so, I stood by the boat, staring into every face, until the last man had gotten off.

Suddenly I felt a poke in my ribs. I swung around to see an old man with a long white beard and a funny hat made from an umbrella.

"Hullo there, Davey," said the Umbrella Man. "Trying to earn a few pennies carrying bags as usual?"

"Hey, there, Mr. Patten," I replied. "You sure don't need your umbrella hat on this pretty day."

Everyone in Seattle called Robert Patten the Umbrella Man. Wearing his odd hat, he earned his living on the streets of Seattle, fixing and selling umbrellas.

The Umbrella Man and I made a good team. When a strong Seattle wind grabbed a lady's umbrella and turned it inside out, I'd bring her to the Umbrella Man so he could fix it. And if the Umbrella Man saw a gent who needed help carrying his bags, he'd holler for me to come do it.

"This here is Davey, sir," he'd say. "He's

an honest boy. For two bits, just a quarter, he'll carry your bags to any hotel in town."

With the help of the Umbrella Man, I'd already saved nine dollars and thirty cents. It was hidden under the floor of the shed, where Mrs. Tinker would never think to look.

I knew I couldn't let Mrs. Tinker know my secret. She might not like me much, but she sure liked all the work I did at her boarding-house. If she suspected I wanted to run away, she'd never let me go to Pioneer Square.

The Umbrella Man beckoned me close. "Davey, have you seen Brownie today? Mark my words, something's up! He rushed by not long ago."

Brownie was Beriah Brown, the star newspaper reporter for the *Seattle Post-Intelligencer*. When something happened in Seattle, Brownie was the first to know.

"Where was he headed?"

"He's down at the docks somewhere. He's trying to charter himself a boat."

"A boat?" I repeated. "Now, why would Brownie need a boat?"

I ran off to find him. It didn't take long. He was shaking hands with a man who looked like a sea captain.

I fell into step beside him as he walked away from the man. "Hey, Brownie. The Umbrella Man tells me you're going to sea. Let me in on the story."

Brownie grinned. "You've got a future as a reporter yourself, kid. There are only a few men in the whole city who know what I'm up to right now. A few men and a ten-year-old boy."

"I'm eleven now," I corrected him. "So what's up?"

Brownie looked around to make sure no one could hear. "I *did* charter myself a tug. It'll take me out tonight to meet a steamboat that's due to arrive in Seattle tomorrow morning."

I stared. "You're going to write a story

about a steamboat? But hundreds of boats come into this port."

"Not like this one. This boat has gold aboard," Brownie whispered, his eyes gleaming.

"Gold!"

Brownie's words spilled out. "I was at the newspaper office when the telegram came from San Francisco. Seems that months ago, a man named George Carmack discovered gold on Bonanza Creek, a tributary of the Klondike River. It's in the Yukon Territory of Canada.

"Now some of the prospectors who struck it rich in the Klondike are coming home. One boat just docked in San Francisco. The other, a steamer called the *Portland,* is on its way to Seattle right now."

Gold! When most folks hear that word, they dream of getting rich. But all I could think of was Uncle Walt. Maybe this was why Uncle Walt hadn't come back. Maybe he'd been prospecting for gold all this time.

Maybe Uncle Walt would be on this steamer. "The *Portland* docks early tomorrow morning," Brownie told me. "But I'm aiming to get the scoop before anyone else. That's why I hired Captain Sprague and the *Sea Lion* to take me out to meet the *Portland* tonight."

Brownie grinned like a little boy about to take a huge bite of chocolate cake. "I'll climb aboard, get the story, and put ashore at Port Townsend to telegraph it back here."

Brownie spread his arms. "Look around you, kid. In the morning this dock will be crowded with thousands, all clamoring to get on a boat headed north. Tomorrow—July 17, 1897—will be a day folks won't forget."

"I want to be here," I told him. "I just have to see those miners get off the boat."

"We're going to publish an early edition of the paper," he replied. "Come down and help sell papers. Kid, tomorrow you'll be part of history."

CHAPTER FOUR

~ Stacks of Yellow Metal ~

"Where are you headed this early, Davey?" Cook whispered as I tiptoed into the kitchen the next morning.

I grabbed a warm biscuit. Cook made the best biscuits in Seattle. "I'm off to help a friend sell newspapers. Oh, and I have to find someone to rent Room Three. I forgot yesterday."

"And you got punished for it too. I don't approve of sending young boys to bed without supper," said Cook with a shake of her head. "Here, take another biscuit. And mind you, be back soon so Mistress don't get angry."

• • •

Outside the newspaper building I spotted my friend Tag, one of the best newsies on the street.

"Hey, Davey, let's head for the docks and sell our extra editions there," he called. "That way we'll get a good spot. I wanna see that gold with my own eyes."

Grabbing all the papers we could carry, we raced to Schwabacher's dock. The morning air felt cool, and I shivered. Or maybe it was just the excitement of seeing Brownie's headline.

"Wow! Tag, did you read this?" I asked.

"Naw, I just heard it was about gold," he replied, taking off his cap to scratch his curly red hair. "I don't read all that good."

"Listen. Here's the headline: 'Gold! Gold! Gold! Gold! Stacks of Yellow Metal!'"

My eyes scanned the paper. "Brownie did it! He got the story on board the *Portland* early this morning."

"Never mind about that," said Tag, pulling

on my sleeve. "Read more about the gold."

"Here's what Brownie says: 'At three o'clock this morning the steamship *Portland* passed up the Sound with more than a ton of gold on board and sixty-eight passengers.'"

Tag's eyes were glued to mine. "A ton of gold! What else?"

I kept reading. "He says the boat has three chests and a safe, all filled with precious nuggets."

Tag gave a low whistle.

"There's more. Listen to this," I went on. "Brownie says 'tenderfeet,' or newcomers, made most of the strikes."

Tenderfeet. That could be Uncle Walt, I figured.

"It's a long way to the gold," I told Tag as I skimmed Brownie's story. "First you have to take a boat along the Inland Passage to Skagway, Alaska. That's eight hundred miles. Then you have to walk over a mountain pass into Canada, thirty miles or so to

Lake Lindeman and the Yukon River. If the Yukon isn't covered by ice, you can travel on it another eight hundred miles, right to Dawson City and the Klondike."

I stopped a minute to catch my breath. "Brownie writes here that a miner needs clothes, supplies, plus a year's worth of grub. The whole outfit costs more than five hundred dollars."

Tag grabbed my arm. "Hey, Davey, didn't you tell me once you had an uncle somewhere up north? Maybe he's on this steamship. Maybe he's already rich."

"I hope you're right, Tag," I said. "Just think, in a little while my uncle Walt might be dragging a sackful of gold off that steamer. Then I'd never have to scrub Mrs. Tinker's parlor floor ever again."

We claimed a spot on the dock and got to work.

"Extra! Extra!" I shouted, until I was

hoarse as a foghorn. "Read all about the gold strike in the Klondike!"

Tag had another method of selling papers. He kept a whistle around his neck. As soon as he blew it, people turned to look. When they did, Tag would wave a newspaper high above his head.

"That's a good way to do it," I said.

"Yeah, I get their attention by whistling so I don't have to yell so loud. My voice was gettin' so that it hurt every day," Tag told me with a grin. He reached into his pocket and tossed me a small tin whistle. "Here, I got an extra. You try it."

But we didn't have time to whistle or call out for long. Soon we were mobbed. People threw coins at me and grabbed papers right out of my hand.

I even got a few tips from folks so excited they started spending money they didn't have.

"Keep the change, lad," said one Irishman. "Before long I'll be buying my newspaper with gold dust."

Within an hour every saloon, boardinghouse, and hotel in town had emptied out. The dock was crammed with men, women, and children, all waiting for their first sight of gold.

"Think it's true?" I heard a man say.

His friend shrugged. "Who knows? Maybe this newspaper fellow made the whole story up, just to sell papers. It's probably a dream. That land up north is all ice and snow."

But I knew better. If Brownie reported a ton of gold, there was a ton of gold.

And gold was what everyone cared about seeing. Well, everyone except me. I just wanted to see my uncle Walt stroll down that gangplank. I wanted to hear his loud laugh and see his brown eyes sparkle.

I couldn't help dreaming about what might happen if Uncle Walt *did* come back a rich man. Maybe he'd take me to live with him in a big, fancy city, like Chicago or San Francisco. Or maybe we'd head back to the Klondike together, to find more gold. I could see myself, a pick in my hand, reaching down into a stream to grab hold of a gold nugget the size of my fist.

All at once a shout went up. "Look, it's here!"

The steamship *Portland* had arrived.

"Darn. I can't see over people's heads. There must be thousands here," cried Tag, jumping up on his toes.

I pointed. "Let's climb onto those crates. We can watch from there."

This is it, I thought. *If Uncle Walt struck it rich he'll be walking down this gangplank, his pockets bulging with gold nuggets.*

When the gangplank was lowered, a hush fell over the crowd. Overhead seagulls cried and squabbled.

The first prospector came into view,

clumping down the wooden gangplank in his hobnail boots. His battered, wide-brimmed hat topped a sunburnt face. The ends of his long gray mustache waved like tiny banners in the breeze.

The miner staggered under the weight of his pack. Could it really be full of gold? Suddenly he stopped, waved his hand in the air, and gave a joyful shout.

"Gold!" he cried. "I'm rich!"

The crowd roared. People pressed forward, eager to talk to the man, ask him questions, or even touch his hand for luck. Before long more miners appeared, dragging bulging suitcases and sacks.

Tag grabbed my arm. "Come on, Davey, let's go. I bet these miners will be looking for a place to stay. We can earn some money carrying bags to hotels. Maybe we'll get paid in gold dust."

I shook my head. "I can't. I want to stay until everyone's off, just in case. . . ."

With a wave Tag jumped down and disappeared into the crowd. From my high perch I watched the miners come off the boat, one by one. I waited until the very end. Uncle Walt never appeared.

"Well, that's that. Uncle Walt must still be up north somewhere," I said out loud. "And I aim to find him."

CHAPTER FIVE

✎ Gold Fever ✎

By the time I clambered down from my hill of crates, I had to push through noisy crowds on every street corner. There were so many people I could barely move. Long lines were already snaking out of every store and steamship ticket office.

Gold fever had struck Seattle.

"Up the Inland Passage to Skagway, Alaska—that's the best way to go. The boats are already filling up," I heard a man yell to his friend. "We gotta get our tickets and our outfit right away. If we don't leave soon, the gold will be gone before we get there."

At the corner of Yesler Way and First Avenue, a mob spilled out of the Cooper and Levy Company. "It's a stampede!" someone hollered in my ear. "They've already sold out of picks, shovels, hatchets, and rubber boots."

Everyone was talking at once. "Where is the Klondike, anyway?" . . . "How do we get there?"

Outside the telegraph office folks lined up to send telegrams to brothers, cousins, and friends all over the country. "Catch the next train to Seattle!" . . . "Send money so I can buy my outfit."

"Men are quitting their jobs right and left," I heard a man say. "I went to the bank to get my money out. When the teller heard the news, he decided to come along as my partner."

Just as I passed the Hotel Seattle, a thin young man with bright blue eyes came out. He looked lost. His shoulders slumped under his heavy pack.

"No rooms left in the whole town," I heard him say to himself. "Where will I sleep tonight?"

Suddenly I remembered Mrs. Tinker's instructions. We still had space at the rooming house. And this young man looked like a decent fellow.

"If you need a place to stay, sir, I can take you to Mrs. Tinker's Rooming House, just up the hill," I told him. "It's clean and we have the best cook in town. I'll even carry your bags for a quarter."

"Why, thank you. I just arrived on the train and heard the news," said the man with a shy smile. "I'll be heading north as soon as I can scrape up the thirty-five dollars for passage to Skagway."

I shouldered the man's pack and led him up the hill. "So you want to find gold, huh?"

The man shook his head and laughed. "Believe it or not, I won't be looking for gold. No, I want to do my own work. I haven't been able to make much of a living anywhere else. Maybe up north it'll be different."

I was curious. "What kind of work do you do?"

"I'm a photographer," he said. "My name is Erik Larsen. I figure folks will want to buy photographs—a record of their adventure."

"I like to draw," I told him.

"You do, eh? Well, photography is an art too, you know. It's a way to capture what you see, to record a moment in time."

"It's hard to capture just one moment in a drawing," I said. "Sometimes when I sketch the harbor, the weather changes before I'm half done. The fog rolls in, thick and heavy, or the rain sweeps down in thick sheets. Nothing stays the same."

Erik Larsen looked at me, his blue eyes twinkling with pleasure. "Ah, but a photograph is magic. It freezes time. Everything changes, yah, but you still have a picture of one moment."

"I think I'd like to try that," I said with a grin.

"Well, maybe you will someday. I can see you're an artist yourself, young man," Erik Larsen went on. "What did you say your name was?"

"Davey. Davey Hill."

The young man held out his hand. "Call me Erik."

We were almost to Mrs. Tinker's when I spotted a man coming out of Mrs. Mac's gate, leading Dandy by a rope.

"Dandy! Where are you taking him, mister? That's Mrs. Mac's horse."

"Not anymore," the man replied. "She just sold him to me for thirty dollars. He's on his way to the Klondike."

Dandy tossed his head and rolled his eyes at me, as if saying good-bye.

Erik Larsen shook his head. "By the end of the week there won't be a horse or dog left in

Seattle. They'll all be sold to prospectors."

Dogs! My heart gave a sudden lurch. I sprinted ahead, even with Erik's heavy pack on my back.

I burst into the kitchen. "Where is he? Where's Joe?"

Cook dabbed at her eyes with the corner of her apron.

"Gone to the Klondike," she said, sniffling. "A man named Crandall spotted him and came to the door to buy him. Mrs. Tinker, she sold him without blinking an eye. I couldn't do anything to change her mind."

"But . . . but Joe is too old to pull a sled, or haul a load through the snow," I stammered.

In the doorway behind me, Erik Larsen cleared his throat. "Begging your pardon, ma'am, but Davey says you might have a room to rent."

"Oh, gracious me, you need to speak with my missus, not me," said Cook, straightening her apron. "I'll take you to her."

• • •

As soon as they went into the parlor to talk to Mrs. Tinker, I ran out to the shed and slipped inside. Crouching, I pried up the loose floorboard. I pulled out the tin can and emptied it. Nine dollars and thirty cents. All I had.

Stuffing the money in my pocket, I raced back to Pioneer Square. It didn't take me long to track down Crandall. He was already camped out in front of the Butler Hotel, surrounded by a bunch of growling, yapping dogs for sale. He must have begun roaming the neighborhoods to buy dogs as soon as he heard the news of the gold strike.

"Just call me the Dog King of Seattle," I heard him boast.

"I'm looking for a big black dog with short hair and sad eyes," I told him. "You bought him from a lady named Mrs. Tinker who runs a rooming house up the hill."

I stood up as tall as I could. "I'm here to buy him back."

The Dog King shrugged. "Maybe I seen a dog like that, maybe I haven't. But if he ain't here, then I already sold him to someone else."

I looked at each and every dog. Joe wasn't there. I wondered if I'd ever see him again.

I trudged slowly up the hill toward home. I couldn't stop thinking about Joe and Dandy. It seemed like gold was already making people crazy.

I spotted Mrs. Mac at her gate as I came up. "Hello, Mrs. Mac. Um . . . I saw that you sold Dandy."

"Oh, what have I done? He just gets me so mad, that horse; I thought it was about time to get rid of him." She sighed. I could see she'd been crying. "But no sooner had the man led him away than my brother came by. He told me any horse taken to the Klondike is sure to be treated horribly."

"Can't you get Dandy back?" I asked.

Mrs. Mac shook her head. "I tried! I'm just on my way home now from talking to that greedy man. But he's already sold Dandy to someone else."

I ducked my head. "Mrs. Tinker sold Joe. I couldn't get him back either."

"That poor, loyal dog?" she cried. She shook her head. "Gold brings out the worst in people, doesn't it? Greed, that's what it is. I'd give anything to take back what I did. But it's too late."

Mrs. Mac seemed sorry for what she'd done. But I didn't think Mrs. Tinker would ever regret selling Joe.

I slipped into the shed and put my money back into its hiding place.

CHAPTER SIX

~ Thief! ~

"Gold! Klondike! Skagway!"
It had been just a few weeks since gold
fever struck, but Seattle was a different place.
Every day more men and women poured off
trains from all over the country. They jammed
the streets to buy supplies, dogs, and horses.

Erik went out to Pioneer Square every
day to take pictures to earn money for his
passage. I was trying hard to get money too.
I'd earned five dollars carrying supplies for
stampeders. Now I had more than fourteen
dollars, but I needed more to buy my boat
passage to Skagway.

One afternoon in early August, Cook sent me to the store. I pushed through Pioneer Square. As usual, it was mobbed with people.

"Which way to the harbor, kid?" someone asked me.

I pointed down the street. "Are you new to Seattle?"

"Yup, just got off the train from Chicago," said the man. "I heard the best route is to Skagway, Alaska, along the Inland Passage. Is that true?"

I nodded. "That's the quickest. But you need a good outfit—enough food and supplies for a year. That's because once you get to Skagway, you have to travel another eight hundred miles into Canada to Dawson."

"The kid's right," said a grizzled old miner who had stopped to listen. "And if you don't leave Seattle soon, you won't get to the Yukon River before it freezes. You'll be stuck at Lake Lindeman until spring. If you can get up the Chilkoot Pass, that is."

"I'm gonna try to find space on a boat right away," said the man from Chicago. "Then I'll buy my outfit, simple as that."

He went off, whistling merrily.

The old miner looked after him and shook his head. "There goes another fool struck by gold fever. Like most of these sourdoughs, he has no idea of the trouble that lies ahead."

The man from Chicago wasn't the only one scrambling to buy supplies. The streets were piled high with goods. New tent stores had sprung up like mushrooms in every alley. On one street the merchants had cut down the trees so they'd have more room to stack goods outside.

"I bought blankets, sleeping bags, and two hundred candles," I heard a man call to his friend. "Any luck with the food?"

The other man nodded. "So far I've got eight hundred pounds of flour, fifty pounds of cornmeal, and two hundred pounds of beans. And I bought fifty pounds of evaporated potatoes at twenty cents a pound."

He looked at a list in his hand. "We still need dried beef, dried apples and peaches, and fifty pounds of coffee."

The man spotted me. "Hey, kid, wanna earn a dime? Carry this sack of rolled oats for us."

Within an hour I'd made fifty cents carrying supplies. Now I had almost fifteen dollars in all. I put the coins in my pocket, went to the market for Cook, and headed home. I didn't dare be late to help serve supper, or Mrs. Tinker would be mad.

When supper was over, I remembered the money in my pocket. Mrs. Tinker and the boarders were sitting at the table, drinking coffee and talking about the Klondike.

This was my chance to hide it.

I slipped outside and into the shed. Kneeling, I pried up the floorboard. It had been a good day. If only I could go out every afternoon, it wouldn't be long before I'd have enough to buy my passage to Skagway—and to leave Mrs. Tinker forever.

Reaching in, I pulled out the tin can where I kept my money.

It was empty.

"Hey, kid. What do you think you're doing?" growled a voice from behind me.

I whirled around. A large man with wide shoulders and stringy black hair loomed in the doorway. He looked like a fierce black bear.

"Get out of this shed," I shouted. My heart beat like a drum inside my chest.

The man laughed and pointed to the corner, where some tools had been cleared out to make way for a sleeping bag and a rucksack.

"I live here now, kid," the man told me with a sly grin. "Mrs. Tinker, she rented this shed to me while I get some supplies together. I'm headed for the Klondike."

The Klondike! I should have known. With every hotel in Seattle full, men were desperate for places to stay. It was a wonder she hadn't kicked me out of my room yet.

I held out the empty can. "What about the money that was in here?"

The man came closer and jutted out his jaw. "Are you calling Big Al a thief, kid?"

I swallowed hard. I just knew this man had searched the shed and taken anything he could find.

I'd never be able to prove Big Al had stolen my money. And Mrs. Tinker wouldn't take my word over his. After all, Big Al was one of her paying boarders.

My heart sank. Everything I had saved was gone.

I ran. I ran as fast as I could, pushing past the man. Up in my room I threw myself down on my cot. All the tears I'd been holding inside for months burst out. I cried for Momma and for Uncle Walt's not coming to get me.

I cried so hard that at first I didn't hear the soft knock on the door. I sat up and wiped my face with the corner of my shirt. Maybe it was Mrs. Tinker. I was too proud to let *her* see me cry.

"Who's there?"

"It's me, Erik."

Erik came in and sat on the edge of my cot. He frowned a little. "Is . . . is everything all right, Davey?"

I shrugged and turned to face the window.

"Look, I just came to tell you I'm leaving for Skagway in a couple of days," said Erik. "I booked passage on the *Al-ki*."

"You're going now? So soon?" I cried. "What about your outfit?"

Erik Larsen shook his head. "I don't need a ton of food and supplies like most prospectors. Remember, I'm not looking for gold. I'll set up shop in Skagway for a while and take

48

photographs of stampeders while they've still got their dreams of being rich."

"Erik, let me come with you," I begged. "Please!"

Erik Larsen paused for a long minute. Then he shook his head. "I wish I could, Davey, but I can't."

"I won't be any trouble, I promise. I'll be your assistant, and you can teach me photography." My words tumbled out. "I'll even help you drum up business. I've sold newspapers, you know. I'll be a big help."

I jumped off the cot and ran to the window. From a nail I grabbed my whistle and blew it. "Hear that? My friend Tag gave me this to help sell newspapers. But we can use it to sell photographs. Whenever I walk through Skagway blowing my whistle, folks will know they can get their pictures taken."

"Davey, I'd be lucky to have a helper like you," said Erik softly. "There's just one problem— I don't have enough money to take care of both of us. Besides, you're just a kid. Look, you've mentioned that your uncle might be up north. But he might be on his way to Seattle right now. What would he do if he got here and found you were gone?"

I shook my head. "I don't think Uncle Walt ever got the letter I sent him. He couldn't have, or he'd have come by now. I just know he's in the Klondike.

"Mrs. Tinker just wants me to work. Cook is nice, but she's not family. I don't want to stay here anymore. Please, Erik. Please take me with you," I begged one last time.

Erik stood up and put his hand on my shoulder. But I already knew what his answer would be.

"I'm sorry, kid," he said.

CHAPTER SEVEN

∽ I Make a New Plan ∾

After Erik left, I went to the window. Beyond the Sound the sun was just sinking, sending streaks of gold across the sky.

Gold! In the last few weeks Seattle and everyone in it had been changed by the promise of riches. The city was so busy, the gold fever so strong, I knew I could earn back all the money I'd lost. It might take me all winter, but I could do it. I could run away next spring.

But could I bear to wait that long?

From my tiny window I saw Erik go out the front door. He liked to take walks in the evening. Suddenly Erik turned and looked up. Seeing me in the window, he smiled, raised his arm, and waved.

Erik Larsen was a good man. I could trust him, I was sure of that.

Suddenly I knew what I had to do.

"You're awful jittery, Davey," said Cook the next morning. "I dropped that little pan and you jumped to the ceiling. Anything on your mind?"

"No, ma'am," I said quickly, but I felt my face turn red. "Cook . . . do you, do you need anything at the store today? I'd like to go down to the harbor."

Cook smiled. "You love to watch boats leave for the Klondike, don't you? Well, I do need some supplies. I'm almost out of coffee and cornmeal. I swear, Big Al is such a bear of a man he'll eat me out of house and home before the week is through!"

I looked out the back window at the shed. "I don't like him much."

"Well, best to stay out of his way," said Cook, counting out some coins and placing them in my hand. "Now get along, before Mrs. Tinker thinks up more chores for you."

The Umbrella Man was in his usual spot in Pioneer Square.

"Have you seen Tag, that newsie with the red hair?" I asked.

"He just trotted off toward Schwabacher's dock, helping some stampeders carry gear to their boat," said the Umbrella Man.

He chuckled. "At least they *called* it a boat. Some of these boats are so low in the water they'll have to bail the whole way to Alaska. And the holds are weighted down with horses and dogs. Poor creatures!"

I nodded. "Brownie says some of these old, leaky boats are sure to end up at the bottom of the Pacific."

"Serves them right, is what I say. Their heads are so full of gold dust they can't think straight. At least sensible folks like us are content to stay right here in Seattle," said the Umbrella Man. "There's money enough to be made here, right, kid?"

"Um . . . right. Well, I better get going." I waved good-bye and headed for the harbor.

I could see a crowd on the dock. People shouted and waved to their friends. "Bring me a stockingful of gold," one shouted.

Near me a mother held up her little girl. "Wave good-bye to Papa, Mary," she said with tears in her eyes. "He's sailing for gold."

I threaded my way to the front of the crowd. Where was he? Suddenly I spotted a flash of red curls under a cap. "Tag!"

"Hullo, Davey. Found your uncle yet?"

I shook my head. "Tag, I need your help."

His eyes widened. "My help? To find your uncle?"

"You might say that." I leaned close. "I can't pay you now, Tag. But maybe . . . maybe

someday I can pay you in gold dust."

"Gold dust! What in the dickens are you talking about, Davey?"

I gulped. "I want to go to Skagway, on the *Al-ki*. It sails the day after tomorrow. But I don't have money or a ticket."

Tag stared at me, his mouth open. His freckles looked as if they might pop right off his face. For a minute I was afraid he'd say I was crazy.

Then his eyes lit up and he broke into a grin. "All right, then. Meet me on the dock tomorrow night."

"What time?"

"Be here at midnight."

I don't know how I got through the next day. I was afraid Mrs. Tinker would suspect I was up to something, so I tried harder than usual to stay out of her way.

I wished I could tell Cook, but I didn't dare. Now that I'd finally made up my mind to go, I realized how much I'd miss her.

"Davey, you've been underfoot all day," Cook remarked.

"Uh . . . sorry," I sputtered. Suddenly I had a thought. "Cook, do you have a real name? A name besides Cook, I mean?"

She laughed and cuffed my ear lightly, sending a spray of flour across my face. "What kind of question is that? Of course I do. My name's Mabel—Mabel Cole."

"Mabel Cole," I repeated. I'd have to remember it so I could send her a letter, or even, someday, a few gold nuggets.

"Davey, why don't you go help that nice Mr. Larsen finish packing. He leaves for the Klondike tomorrow morning, you know."

I shook my head. "No! He'll probably want me to help carry his bags tomorrow morning, and I won't do that, either. Let him find someone else."

Cook stopped, mixing spoon in the air, and stared at me. "Why, Davey Hill, you sound like you've been drinking vinegar. What has Mr. Larsen done to cause you to be so bitter? I thought you two were friends."

"We're not. And you can tell him that too. The sooner he's out of this rooming house, the happier I'll be."

I turned on my heel and stomped up the stairs. Later in the evening, when Erik Larsen came to say good-bye, I turned my face to the wall and refused to talk to him. It pained me to imagine the hurt look on his face—but what else could I do?

I had to make everyone believe I was too upset with Erik to see him off at the dock. And I certainly didn't want Erik asking for my help carrying his bags. Because early tomorrow morning, when Erik Larsen boarded the *Al-ki,* there would be no way I could help carry his bags.

I would already be on the boat.

CHAPTER EIGHT

～ Midnight on the Dock ～

"Don't dawdle, boy. Clear the gentlemen's dishes!" ordered Mrs. Tinker when supper was over.

I thought she'd never stop giving me chores to do. But finally I managed to escape to my room.

All I wanted to do was sleep, but I didn't dare lie down for even a minute. What if I didn't wake up in time?

Instead I got ready. I pulled out my old rucksack from under my cot. I stuffed my winter jacket inside, along with extra socks, underwear, pants, and shirts. I took

Momma's wooden box, with her letters and the only photograph I had of her. There was enough room for my wool blanket. I slipped the whistle Tag had given me into my pocket.

I couldn't go without my pencils and sketchbook. As I went to put them in a sheet of paper slipped to the floor. It was a sketch of Cook I'd done one rainy morning as she was kneading bread. It wasn't very good, but at least I'd been able to capture the twinkle in her eye.

What would Cook think when she found out I was gone? I knew she'd be worried. But I still didn't dare tell her the truth. After all, she was a grown-up, and she might feel obliged to tell Mrs. Tinker.

All at once I had an idea. Grabbing my pencil, I wrote on the bottom of the sketch: *Mabel Cole, Best Cook in Seattle, drawn by David Hill, age 11, 1897.*

I didn't own a watch, but that didn't

matter: Mrs. Tinker went to bed every night at ten o'clock sharp. As she said good night to the boarders, her shrill voice carried through the house, even to the attic. I opened my door and stood on the landing to listen.

"Good night, gentlemen. And good luck to you, Mr. Larsen," she said.

"Don't forget *me*, Mrs. Tinker," said a deep voice. "I'm headed to Skagway on the *Al-ki* too."

I froze, barely able to breathe. Big Al! He would be on the very same boat. But I wasn't about to back out now.

I waited until the house was dark and still. Holding my shoes in one hand and my pack in the other, I tiptoed down the stairs in my stocking feet.

First I stopped in the kitchen. I knew Cook wouldn't mind if I took some leftover biscuits and dried apples. Then I made my way to the back of the house.

The sounds of gentle snoring came from Cook's room. "Good-bye, Cook," I whispered. "I hope I see you again."

Then I slipped the sketch under her door and was gone.

On the dock I crouched out of sight behind a wooden post. The minutes dragged. What if Tag forgot?

All at once he was beside me. "You ready, kid?" he whispered, grinning.

I nodded. My teeth were chattering, but not from cold.

"What now?" I whispered back.

"Some of the freight has already been loaded. When you get on board, find a place below to hide," Tag told me.

He pointed to the old freighter, bobbing gently at the dock. "I'm pretty sure there's just this one old guy on guard. I'll go over there and distract him. When he leaves his post, make a run for it."

I gulped. "But . . . but how do I know he'll leave?"

"Don't worry, he will. You can do it, kid." Tag clapped his hand on my shoulder. "When the time is right, creep up, hiding behind whatever you can. Then make your move."

Without another word Tag slunk off, moving like a cat. I crept forward, hiding behind a few barrels and crates. I was close enough to see the guard, a thin man with a white mustache that shone in the glow of his lantern.

I held my breath and listened as hard as I could. All I could hear was the lapping of the water against the dock.

I put my hand over my heart, but it wouldn't stop pounding. *What if the guard catches me?* I thought. *What if I can't hide in time?*

All at once the silence was broken by a crash, then a thud.

"Help! Oh, please help me!" Tag's yell came sharply across the dock.

The guard jerked to attention. "Who's there?"

"Over here! Over here! Ouch, it hurts. My ankle!"

For a second I smiled, imagining Tag writhing on the ground, pretending to be hurt. The guard must have been a kind-hearted man. He took off in a run to where Tag lay buried under crates and boxes.

Now! I told myself. *Run, now!*

Without looking back, I made a dash for the boat.

CHAPTER NINE

∽ Sailing for Gold ∽

Faster, faster, faster . . .

Clomp! Clomp! My feet flew across the wooden planks. Once I stubbed my toe on a coil of rope and almost tripped. At last I scrambled on board.

I looked back. The old man with the mustache was still out of sight behind a hill of crates, bent over Tag. Now I just needed a good place to hide.

It wasn't easy to find my way in the dark. Already the deck of the old freighter was piled high with gear, crates, and coils of rope. And most of the stampeders hadn't loaded their outfits yet. *How would everything fit?* I wondered.

Crouching down, I snaked through the maze. I would have only a few minutes before the guard came back.

There—a ladder! I put my foot on the top rung and swung my leg around. I climbed down, below deck. I'd be less likely to be discovered there.

I figured at first everyone would stay on deck, waving good-bye to friends and family and watching Seattle fade into the distance.

Of course, I knew I wouldn't be able to stay hidden for six days and nights. Sooner or later I'd have to come out and show myself to Erik Larsen. I just wanted to be as far from Seattle as possible when I did.

And I didn't want Big Al to find me first.

Down below I could see berths strung up in every available space, three or even four on top of one another. The passengers wouldn't be very comfortable in this old boat. But most stampeders wouldn't care about that. After all, it was "Klondike or bust!"

In one corner of the lower deck I found a large wooden chest, piled high with old gear, rain jackets, rope, and life preservers. It didn't look as if anyone had touched it in a long time.

I can hide in here, I thought. *I'll pull this rope and the old rain slickers right over my head.*

Climbing inside, I made a nest in the bottom of the chest, inside the coils of rope. The rope scratched my skin and smelled like the sea, but I didn't care.

I just hope I don't get too seasick, I thought grimly.

I'd tucked everything inside and was arranging my pack against my head when I heard footsteps. The guard!

"Fool boy," I heard him mutter.

I froze and tried not to breathe. What if the guard suspected what Tag had really

been up to? How carefully would he search?

In the darkness above me I could see patches of light and shadow. The footsteps came closer. Then they stopped.

The man coughed. My heart pounded. I heard a clinking sound. He had put the lantern down, right near my hiding place.

"Aahchoo!" The man sneezed. Then he blew his nose loudly. I grinned. He'd stopped to take out his handkerchief, that was all.

In a minute the guard picked up the lantern and left. I was alone. Below me the old freighter bobbed in the water like a contented duck. And somehow I drifted off to sleep.

Clomp! Clomp!

I woke with a start. Footsteps!

Close by a gruff voice called, "Well, partner, I guess we'll be sleeping down here."

"Not me. Most likely by nightfall I'll be on deck, sick as a dog," a man answered with a laugh.

At first I didn't remember where I was. Then it all came back. In my shadowy hiding place I stretched my legs as much as I could without making a noise.

I guessed it was early morning, just after dawn. The *Al-ki* would be leaving soon. The first passengers were coming on board and loading their gear.

Before long the boat was bursting with shouts and laughter. Men panted and huffed as they loaded crates and boxes. Dogs barked and horses neighed. The *Al-ki* was no longer silent. It had become a bustling, noisy place.

To my surprise I heard a girl's voice. "Look, Ma, little bunks to sleep in! Won't it be fun?"

I hadn't expected that there'd be other kids on board. I wondered if I'd have the chance to meet them, or whether I'd be discovered and thrown off first.

Suddenly I felt a lurch. The boat had broken free of its ropes. Above me, from the boat and the dock, the shouts grew louder.

"Good-bye and good luck," people hollered.

All at once I heard a familiar loud whistle. From the dock Tag's voice came clear and loud. "Hurray for the Klondike Kid!"

Deep in my hiding place I grinned from ear to ear.

We were off!

No matter what happened next, at this moment I was happy.

I had done exactly what I'd set out to do. I had run away from Mrs. Tinker, and I'd never go back. I might be alone, but I had a plan. I was on my way to the Klondike at last. I would join Erik Larsen, and I'd do my best to find Uncle Walt.

I was sailing for gold.

To be continued . . .

Ho, for the Klondike! The three books in this series, The Klondike Kid, chronicle a great American adventure: the Klondike Gold Rush. Although Davey Hill and other main characters are fictional, many of the details and minor characters are based on factual events and real people.

Word of a gold discovery by George Carmack and others on August 17, 1896, on Rabbit Creek, a tributary of the Klondike River in Canada, didn't reach the outside world until the next year. The country was in an economic depression, with many people out of work. Thousands caught gold fever. When the steamship *Portland* docked in Seattle in July 1897, word of its cargo electrified the city. A newspaper reporter named Beriah Brown ("Brownie" in this story) sailed out to meet the boat, and the Seattle *Post-Intelligencer* printed these headlines:

GOLD! GOLD! GOLD! GOLD!
68 RICH MEN ON THE STEAMER PORTLAND.
STACKS OF YELLOW METAL!

Five thousand people greeted the *Portland* when it docked on July 17, 1897. The crowd watched in amazement as miners dragged suitcases, sacks, and blankets full of gold nuggets and dust down the gangplank.

This news had a big impact on the city of Seattle. By mid-morning the downtown streets were jammed with people. The crowds were so thick streetcars had to stop running. In the coming months, thousands more made their way to Seattle, which became the primary jumping-off point for hopeful prospectors wanting to travel to the Klondike.

But just getting to the Klondike was a feat in itself. Men and women had to buy enough supplies and food to last a year. They had to book passage north, then journey hundreds of miles in harsh conditions. The trails to the Klondike are the stuff of legend: the grueling, icy Chilkoot Pass, and the horror of White Pass, or "Dead Horse Trail."

Most of those who rushed to the Klondike met with disappointment. Some gave up before they reached the boomtown of Dawson City. Most who made it that far learned that the richest stakes had been claimed long ago. The Klondike Gold Rush did not last long. In 1899 word came of a gold strike in Nome, and the Klondike Gold Rush began to fade. But this last great adventure continues to capture our imaginations.

FURTHER INFORMATION

There are many valuable Internet sites on the Klondike Gold Rush. Here are just a few:

For further information about Seattle's role, visit the Klondike Gold Rush Seattle Unit, National Historical Park, either in person or on the Internet at http://www.nps.gov/klse. The National Park Service also maintains a Klondike Gold Rush National Historical Park in Skagway, Alaska. Visit it on the Internet at http://www.nps.gov/klgo.

For resources and curriculum materials, including many primary historical documents, visit the University of Washington's Klondike Gold Rush Web site at http://www.washington.edu/uwired/outreach/cspn/curklon/main.html.

ACKNOWLEDGMENTS

Special thanks to the library staff in special collections at the University of Washington, to the rangers at the Klondike Gold Rush Seattle Unit, and to author Melanie J. Mayer for her advice and the invaluable interviews she donated to the University of Washington from her book *Klondike Women: True Tales of the 1897-1898 Gold Rush*.